Nadia Hears the Shahadah

This book belongs to:

_____

In the name of The Most Gracious, The Most Merciful ...
Only with His permission.
With love and support from my husband and from our children Jalal, Jasmine, Bashier, and Nadia.
With inspiration from my dear friend Margaret Norman.
With insight and invaluable input from Jasmine Baten.
With patience and amazing talent from Marisa Lu.
With the foundation of strong faith from my parents.
May He guide us all.

- K.N.B.

Kim Nisha Baten was born in Canada and has lived in Maryland most of her life. She was raised under another religion, and then found the tranquility and beauty of Islam after marrying into the religion. She is a mother of four, an active volunteer in her children's schools, and a pediatrician. Her wish is to help others better understand the religion of Islam from a simple perspective. With this book, it is her dream to educate and inspire the young and old, those who have newly found Islam, and those who wish to learn about Islam.

Marisa Lu is currently a Design and Human-Computer Interaction double major at Carnegie Mellon University. She was a fanatic doodler as a kid, dreamed of being a concept artist, and now applies her fine art background in rapid prototyping and visualizing for her design projects, research for speech-driven animated books, and of course, the occasional illustration commission. Future plans include building a tiny house on wheels and painting on the go when not in school or at work.

Nadia hears the Shahadah

Written by

Kim Nisha Baten

Illustrated by

Marisa Lu

Published by Tughra Books
335 Clifton Ave.
Clifton, NJ, 07011, USA
www.tughrabooks.com
Library of Congress Call Number (LCCN) 2018023986

Nadia Hears the Shahadah

Written by Kim Nisha Baten

Development Editing by Jasmine Baten

Illustrations by Marisa Lu

ISBN 9781597849340

Printed in China

بسم الله الرحمن الرحيم

In the Name of God, the All-Merciful, the All-Compassionate

Jasmine is putting on her *Hijaab*. That's the pretty scarf she is wearing. Jasmine is my big sister. She's beautiful and really smart. She knows how to do *Salaat* really well. That's what we call our prayers.

It is time to go to the *Masjid*. The *Masjid* is a place where we can do our *Salaat*. Today is Friday, *Jumu'ah*, the best day of the week.

We get to the *Masjid* in plenty of time. The *Imam* is already saying something. He's the nice man who always leads the prayer.

What is he saying? Why is everyone smiling?
Is that lady crying?

Mommy is explaining to Jasmine that today someone will be saying the *Shahadah* for the first time.

The *Shahadah*? What is that? What does that mean? Will somebody please tell me what is going on!

Oh, wait. Let me listen to Mommy. "When somebody has found the Peace of God in their heart, they say the *Shahadah* to become a new brother or sister of Islam. Let's listen…"

"Ash-hadu al laa ilaaha ill Allah, wa ash-hadu anna Muhammadar rasool ullah."

Jasmine is asking Mommy
what that means.

"It means that I bear witness that there is no god except Allah (or there is only one God), and I bear witness that Muhammad (peace be upon him) is His messenger."

Everyone is so happy for our new Muslim brother.

I like the *Shahadah*. I want to learn how to say it too, just like our new Muslim brother. I know I have Islam in my heart. Maybe *insha'Allah*, someday soon, when I learn to talk, I will say the *Shahadah* just as beautifully.

Now, let's see what we have learned

Allah: God

Hijaab: headscarf

Imam: a man who leads the Muslim prayer

Insha'Allah: God willing

Jumu'ah: Friday, the day Muslims gather at the mosque for a special noon-time prayer

Masjid: mosque, a place Muslims gather to pray

Salaat: prayer

Shahadah: Saying that there is no god but Allah, and Muhammad (peace be upon him) is His Messenger.